LASER WOMAN - THE FOUNT

LIFE OF A DEPRESSED

LUCIUS MAURICE ' DAKSH '

I would like to dedicate this book for all of them who supported my writings . Thank you all of you .

Contents

Preface

This book is written to enrich the imagination of children . It is second in the series of superheros . So do enjoy it .

Also By The Author

A.S. Potter - The Whole Timeline

- Zooba - The Rise
- Zooba - The King of the Zoo
- Gravity Man - The Commencement
- Bed Wars - But people die

CHAPTER ONE

My life

I was just going to my dormitory when I saw those bully girls who were always bullying newbies and doing boistrous things . It seemed boring , I never tried to join them . I got in my room 526 . There it was Olga sitting at a chair and a book at a table named - ‘ The Idiot . ’ I did n’t knew much about it except it a romantic book concerned with a love triangle . She asked , " Is your sister alright , Alina ? " She was reffering to my little 5 year old sister . She was lying in the nearby govt. hospital . I was just very sad for her . The moments I spent with her . She was laughing when I had my nose brown when eating a Icecream . Her sad face when she came to knew that I have failed in a surprise test . That all thing came at once to my mind . I replied , " Yeah , she is fine . The Doctor said that she would be fantastic till next month if she would be good taken care of . " Olga thought for a moment ans then said , " You are saying this from the last year . Your stepfather too did not look you after . He only sent you a letter and some few hundred rubles . " Yeah , he married my mother I guess almost 6 years ago . He was very kind to her and very unfair to me . But I did not mind it because when I saw my mother happy my all sadness would be gone . After that , my mother died . He was offered a job faraway in a city of Moscow as a accountant , unable to get all expenses there he left them here in Uglich . I just cannot figure out why all the sad moments were I remembering now . I said , " I am going out to get some fresh air . I turned for the door . Olga exclaimed , " Alina , come back till 7 . " I nodded and got out of that dorm . I sat under my favourite tree and was just thinking is life fair to me ? Must I study hard to get me and my sister a better future . Suddenly , a advertisement paper bumped my face . I was just gonna throw it when I saw that military was doing a experiment in which harmful rays would be emitted and the one who will survive will get a million rubles . I was just gonna call when I saw the surviving chances which were 5 % . I was shocked . Between all this I got a call . " Is this Ms. Alina Pushkov talking ? " I replied in a confused tone, " Yup , who is this ? " " It is Uglich Govt Hospital here . Your sister Anya Pushkov's condition is going worst . She just have two days left with her that too with help of a harmful chemical . That chemical would have no effect if after that the operation is done with the modest fee . "

CHAPTER TWO

Met my love

" I now scared after listening whole this exclaimed , " How much money needed for the operation ? " The guy on the call said , " Wait a sec . " The call was on hold then after a minute he said , " It is a 100,000 rubles . " I was shocked to hear that . I cannot get any help from any side . If I wrote a letter to my stepfather , it would reach to him a week later . I have to get money from somewhere . My mind was puzzled . Then I remembered that experiment and rushed to the phone booth . I remembered the number and called ' 1973540 ' It processed out . Those were the most awkward moments of my life . My mind was burstling with pain , my heart was pounding hard , a cold sweat just trickled on my back as a voice came back from it . " It's Russian Military talking . Who is this ? " I unable to get voice out of my throat said , " It's Alina here . I just read a ad in which you were gonna award the survivor a million rubles . " There was a pause as she was getting me and then came the answer . " Yes , it will happen tommorow , the survivor will be kept under observation for a day and after that is he/she is alright we discharge them . Do you wanna participate ? " I was not listening her . I was just remembering all important people of my life . My mom , my dad , my sister , Olga and my crush Logan . But now , it was a moment to decide . I had a second in which I have to take the most important decision of my life . Everything was being entangled . My ambitions , my books , my best friends and of course, Logan . But a unusual force forced me to say something . A voice struck out of my dried mouth and soft , tender lips- " Yes . " She uttered , " Tommorow afternoon 3 p.m. in Rostov . " I cried whole night that day because I knew tommorow can be the last day of my life .

Next day , I wore a black jacket and a pink skirt . I took a backpack with a water bottle and a tiffin inside . I bid goodbye to Olga who always been nice to me . I got on to the military base . In the streets , when I was gonna get to the Subway , I bumped with some boy . I was just gonna apolozise when I saw who was it - Logan . He had grey eyes , his skin was white . His hair were not well combed . He wore a homemade sweater and some dirty pajamas . Still , he was looking awesome . He got up gave me his hand to stand up , gathered my belongings , gave it to me and ran . I figured out he was in a hurry . I just walked they could be the last moments of my life , but seeing Logan I did not know why but yeah , I smiled .

But that smile was short-lived because when I turned with the intention of seeing him I found him talking with some girl . He had his hand around her waist . I came to know he was in no hurry . But I hurried because I don’t wanna kill myself before the experiment or I would not get the money to cure my sister .

CHAPTER THREE

Saved ... but ?

I entered the military camp and I found it very , very large . There it was an isolation chamber . It was particularly made of iron . It had many equipments inside it . I was just very nervous . I can feel my blood being circulated very fast . They first made me wear another clothes . I cannot figure out why it is important . I was made stand in a queue . There were I guess 37 applicants . I was at the 34th place . Still , I chatted with some same girls of my age who were standing beside me . The first girl was Zarah . She was doing it because his big stepbrother forced him to do so. He wanted drugs . For them , he would have killed her . To save her life , she was there . Her place was 35th . Second girl was Viviana . She was doing it because she wanted to experience what it felt like inside that thing . Her place was 36th . The third and last girl was Tansy . She was her because she had nothing left in her life except poverty . She could not even get 2 time food to survive . She was here because she wanna die . Her place was the last 37th .

We talked continuously for about half an hour . Every 37 seconds a dead body would go from our side , we would get nervous and talk more and more . We noticed it would decrease our anxiety . At last , it was my turn . I gave a hug to my newly made friends and got inside the chamber still thinking about Logan . I got in the chamber . I realized they were emitting a special type of lasers on me I punched kicked the chamber but no luck.

I got unconscious . When I got up , I found that I was in my home . I searched for the money but nope . I got to the bank to collect the money sent by my stepfather . I told my name and was just counting the rubles when the counterperson asked , " Are you Alina Pushkov ? " I wondered how she knew my name ? I nodded . " You have a account with 5 million rubles in it . Still we need your signature . Can we ? " I was shocked to hear that . I just stammered and asked , " How ? " She first presented the form to me , gestured me to sign and said , " Someone came , opened your bank account and deposited the money . I withdrawed a hundred thousand rubles and rushed to the hospital . I got to the counter . " I have to deposit some money for my sister Anya Puhkov's operation . But before it can I meet her ?" She curled her lips and said , " Room no. 510 " I said , " No , you are confused her room number was317.

CHAPTER FOUR

I destroyed a hospital

She was gonna shift to 482 . Still I was asked by the doctor to ask you first . " She looked up , just touched her eyes a little and said , " Sorry , but we don't keep dead bodies in Room no 482 i.e. Pre- op area . " I just said , " No , what do you mean ? " She said , " Your sister is in Room no. 510 which is Mortuary . " I asked in a nervous tone , " What you do in mortuary ? " She said something which took the soul out of me , " Place where corpses means dead bodies are kept . " I just smiled and asked , " Are you telling me that my sister is dead ? " She just glanced at the floor and said , " Yes . " I just fall and screamed with all of my might , " What you doctors were doing then ? You just let my sister die ? " The guards threw me out of the hospital then . I just focused , pointed my hands to the hospital sign and was just gonna say some cursing words when I heard some unusual voice . It was like a Motorbike going at full speed . I opened my eyes and found some pink like structure of light hit that sign and the next moment I knew it were lasers . I again got in , signed the form and vowed that I would always try to save people with this ability of mine.

But police was already behind me . I took my sister in my arms and just ran trying to save myself from their bullets by throwing every object possible in front of their car so they would slow down and it worked . With my ability , I threw a pole in front of them and they stopped . I got in Room 526 . It was again Olga reading the same book . But now the room seemed a little tidy . As I gon in with a thump she was just startled . " What are you d...... ." Before she can complete her sentence she heard the police sirens and she knew they got Alina .

For the next three days , media covered the incident at hospital continuously and police searched the area again and again . The whole city of Uglich was just astonished . Debates were going on tv . Everyone was making some rough guess . But Alina knew whole reality . She had to do something .

CHAPTER FIVE

Some moments with Logan

Next day , I got to the military camp , breaking all the rules , I got in and asked to the head of that camp , " Who held that experiment ? " He just showed me his fake eye and when he got to know I was determined he told me , " Mr Ross . " I got the taxi , still with the guilt of my sister being dead . I reached the airport . I was now rich . So , there was no problem to get to Manila , Phillipines where he is gonna deliver a speech . I sat in the aeroplane for the first time , I hold my seat like as a child . I was so nervous . I was sweating . I don't know how but after that I got a nap . When I woke up , it were 15 minutes in the air . I gazed on my hand , they were on some man's . I looked forward to the person . I had my mouth open . It was Logan . He was wearing some headphones of the famous company Cowin . Between all this , his background remebered by me . His father was the Governor of a state Yaroslavl Oblast . He studied in an international in St. Peterberg .I studied with him in grade 12th . He was listening to some nice song named Elinka which I listened when I was in 3rd grade . He was awake , moving his jaw like he was singing . He gazed upon me , I still like frozen . He unbanded his headphones

, thrusted his hand forward and said which I was like I have to listen from that one year . Everday I felt like it whenever he passed from my side , " Hi Alina Pushkov , I am Logan Kuzumich . " I sent my hand forward to his like he was proposing me and I was giving my hand forward like I wanted him to push the ring in my Ring finger . We then talked like for two hours and I was busy seeing him like yeah , I cannot explain . I did not realized when the flight ended . He told me he was also going to the Manila . We again sat in a taxi . He was just talking when I laid my head on his chest . I can feel his heartbeat . He was nervous . But hen he hugged me and that were the golden moments of my life . I can hear people outside saying Phillipian and saying us I don’t know what and what . But yeah , we were lost in our own world .

CHAPTER SIX

I was taken to Malina

I booked a room in hotel where he was staying . We had dinner together , then a glass of red wine and we departed to our rooms . I made my mind to ready to meet Mr Ross tommorow . I slept but around 3 hours later I found I being woke up by Logan . " Alina wake up , Alina , Alina ! " We made our way to outside of the hotel . But still I can hear people trapped in the hotel . Suddenly , one side of the hotel fall . I can see some children there crying . I vowed and to continue it , I need to go there and save them but how flying ? Of couse not ! " You would return these to me after it is over . " I gazed to Logan . He had opened a briefcase which contained some pressure giving instruments which can be applied to the hands and feet. I was astonished . " How ? " He replied , " I will explain later . " I just got it said out of excitement , " It's astounding . " But suddenly, I noticed that a wall was gonna fall on the small angels . I just flew there , got them into my lap and flew down . All were just praising me . Suddenly , some wall fall above me and I just got my hands up and yeah , disolved it in into small pieces . Then , Logan got my hand made me sat in a E-Class Sedan . He got out to sit in the front seat , but mediaperson surrounded him . " Sir who is she ? A criminal or a justice proivider? " He just wore his sunglasses and replied in an irony voice , "

We will inform you later . " But just then a reporter jumped forward and asked , " Sir , just tell us what was that light ? " He opened the door and said before sitting , " Those were lasers emitted by this woman's hands." I was taken to Malina , where Mr Ross was gonna deliver a speech . After about half an hour later , Mr Ross sat in front of me and said

CHAPTER SEVEN

I met Mr Ross but he is a psycho

" Let me introduce myself . I am Ronald Ross . I am the owner of Ross Industries . I have brought you here regarding some important unofficial but classified matter . " I protested , " Let me go . " He slided his laptop in front of me . " The experiment was done by me . As you know our body is a conductor of energy . So , when that harmful rays were emitted on you . Your body stored that energy and now you are Laser Woman . A terrorist is there who had build a machine through which he want to take energy out of Earth . He planned to take one-fourth part out of this planet . " I questioned , " What he would get for it ? " He walked on to the laptop , opened something and said , " This person is Wong Zang . He is a businessan, he is very passionate about his collection of artefacts . He wants that thing . He have many thousand billion dollars and has announced that he would give the person many many money who would bring him that energy . Now , for that he hired this terrorist to make a machine get it out. Now the name of that terrorist is Danny . Wong Zang is nowadays active in National Intelligence Coordinating Agency because Danny wants him to erase his info . Now , you can go . " I called on to him . " Wait , I want to help but of no use . " I tried to remember everything he told me and I got it . I passed the gate by making the guard unconscious for about an hour .

CHAPTER EIGHT

Sneaked into NICA and got a surprise too

I searched whole files of NICA . At last , I got on to a computer . I searched ‘ Danny . ’ There it was . I found where he was . I got a print of it . I got pushed from behind by someone and I got bumped into a glass window . I looked behind , it was my stepfather . I for the first time in my life ran to him and hugged him . But he just parted me from him . " Who are you , intruder ? " Some tears dropped on the ground . " Alina Pushkov . " His eyes just were big . I explained him the whole issue . He just gave me some Phillipine Paso . After a hug , when I was going , " Stop . " I was wondering what my Dad want to tell me now .He just showed me a Ruby ring . " This is the ring your real Dad gave to your mom . I don’t know that ever will I be able to give you the same love he would have gave you if he was alive but I tried my best . This is the best I can do . " I just took that ring from him , gave him a hug but this time with my heart and my love . " Just go . " I nodded and I waved him bye . I just jumped down this time rented a Marrousi and just gone towards the Phillipine Trench . I just knew what to do . It was 2:30 p.m. I boarded a boat towards the Northern direction . At a place , the boat begun to turn . I yelled , " Hey ! I want to go further . " The boatman replied , " Further is a dangerous terrorist's area . "

CHAPTER NINE

I am caught

I just jumped off the boat without anyone notice . That man had his own St Peterberg 5 star cruise . I was just astonished . I entered the place where the water was kept because I was feeling very thirsty . " Who are you ? " came a voice from behind . I turned and found a black person standing beside me . I knew I was caught . I was taken to Danny . He was also a black person . Except the fact his eyes were irony grey . He was wearing a leather shower robe which was looking very odd fashioned . " Boss , see who is here , a girl intruder . " He turned and I was just scared to see him . There was a big scar near his eye . He was drinking some alochol and he wore a gold chain which was definitely real . " Ah ! The tricks of that fucking agency . Now , you know what to do . Take her to that room . " The soliders nodded and I was taken to a room where was just a bed . I was thrown there and about 2 minutes later , he came and said , " A night with you and then you will be executed . " He was just coming very near to me . If I wanted I would have killed him with the lasers but it would have destroyed the whole ship killing me and all of the agents of NICA kept in the basement . I knew there was no way out .

CHAPTER TEN

Logan , my love

But suddenly , there was a explosion in the wall of the room and some man came in . " She is mine and you said that bad words now you will pay for it . " It was Logan . He reloded his PDW Semi-22 and just fired at him . But he took a cover behind the bed and was saved . I did not figured out what was happening . There was continuous firing for about 15 minutes . After that , Danny got a bullet . Logan just came to me , got me up and we were just gonna exit from the place when I saw behind Danny was taking a pistol in his hand and his aim was Logan . " Careful . " I screamed . I just tried to fire lasers at him but a pink crystal just hit him and his body vanished leaving his skeleton aside . I was unconscious then . Last thing I saw was that Logan running to me .

CHAPTER ELEVEN

I got a Date

I woke up . I saw Mr Ross and Logan in front of me . Mr Ross opened his mouth to say but I interrupted , " You done what you can . " He just smiled and said , " Of course . " In years first time I saw Logan was holding my hand . " Would you like to have a coffee with me ? Beautiful Lady . " I displayed a grin , " Why not ? " Mr Ross laughed and then continued , " Here it is . A suit for you and that flying equipments . You deserve it . Now what with Wong Zang ? " I displayed my sinister smile , " Can you turn on the television?" It was done and what the people in the whole room saw got their eyes out . Breaking News - Wong Zang is dead because of eating some poisonous things here . In the past , when Alina was searching for the docs she saw a coffee full cup with the name - Wong Zang . She mixed some poison in it . The result was in front of eyes . He was dead . Logan said , " You are just fantastic . " I smiled , " Now your secrets . " He looked at the ground and then answered , " I work for Mr Ross . I am a special agent of his and that flying equipments are made by me . Leave it . Would you like to go on a date with me ? Let me introduce myself . I am Logan Lerman . " I was happy and said , " I am Al... . " I paused , thought and said , " I am Laser Woman . "

Going Back

The ring given by my mother was just kept near my table , I wore it . After spending a marvellous day with Logan I decided to go back Russia via Japan with my flying equipments . So , I just flew when I was flying I saw some nerd looking up at me but I did not care because I knew I had my life .

9 798887 045283

Printed by Libri Plureos GmbH in Hamburg,
Germany